Horace Bushnell

The Insight of Love

Horace Bushnell

The Insight of Love

ISBN/EAN: 9783337331801

Printed in Europe, USA, Canada, Australia, Japan

Cover: Foto ©Andreas Hilbeck / pixelio.de

More available books at **www.hansebooks.com**

The Insight of Love

Horace Bushnell *

1892

"She hath done what she could; she is aforehand to anoint my body to the burying."—MARK xiv, 8.

It takes a woman disciple after all to do any most beautiful thing; in certain respects too, or as far as love is wisdom, any wisest thing. Thus we have before us, here, a simple-hearted loving woman, who has had no subtle questions of criticism about matters of duty and right, but only loves her Lord's person with a love that is probably a kind of mystery to herself, which love she wants somehow to express. She comes therefore with her box of ointment, having sold we know not what article, or portion of her property, to buy it, for it was very costly, and pours it on the Saviour's head—Just here to encounter, for

---

*"The Insight of Love," in *Sermons on Christ and His Salvation* (New York: Charles Scribner's Sons, 1892), 51–70. Original version available on the Internet Archive. This version updated September 19, 2017.

the first time, scruples, questions, and rebuffs of argument. For though she is no casuist herself, no debater of eases of conscience, there are abundance of such among the Lord's male disciples present, Judas among them, and they have more reasons, a great many, to offer than she, poor child of love, has ever thought of. "Hold woman," they say, and particularly Judas in the representation of John, "Why this extravagance and foolish waste? Is not the Lord always teaching us to consider the poor, and do good in every thing, and what immense good might you have done, had you sold this ointment and put it to the uses of beneficence; why, the trains of benefit you might have set agoing by the money are even endless, and now it is thrown away for just nothing." She makes no answer, has nothing at all to say, and does not see, most likely, why she has not been as foolish as they think.

But Christ answers for her. "No, children, no," he says, "do not trouble the woman, she has an oracle in her love wiser than yours that you have in your heads; she has done a good work on me, fitting, altogether, to be done by her, if not by you. Nay, she has even prophesied here, taken hold practically of my future—just that which I have never been able to make you conceive, or guess. The poor you have always with you, be it yours to bless them, but me ye have not always. She is come aforehand—dear prophetic tribute!—to anoint my body for the burying. Is it nothing that I die in the fragrant odors of this dear woman's love? Verily I say unto you,

wheresoever this gospel shall be preached through-
out the whole world, this also that this woman bath
done, shall be told for a memorial of her."

No such commendation was ever before or after
conferred by the Saviour on any mortal of the race.
He testified for the Gentile centurion, that he had
found no such faith as his even in Israel. He tacitly
commended his three favorite disciples, Peter, James
and John, by the peculiar confidence into which he
took them. But the little gospel, so to speak, of this
loving woman's devotion, he declares shall go forth 53
with his, to be spoken of, and felt in its beauty, and
breathed in its fragrance, in all remotest regions of
the world, and latest ages of time.

And what is the lesson or true import of this so
much commended example? What but this?—do for
Christ just what is closest at hand, and be sure that
you will so meet all his remotest, or most unknown
times and occasions. Or, better still, follow without
question the impulse of love to Christ's own person;
for this when really full and sovereign, will put you
along easily in a kind of infallible way, and make
your conduct chime, as it were, naturally with all
God's future, oven when that future is unknown; un-
tying the most difficult questions of casuistry without so much as a question raised.

And precisely here, not elsewhere, is the great
contribution Christ has made to morality, or the
department of duty. He inaugurates, in fact, a new
Christian morality, quite superior to the natural
ethics of the world. Not a new morality as respects

the body of rules, or code of preceptive obligations,
though even here he instituted laws of conduct so
important as to create a new era of advancement,
but new in the sense that he raised his followers to
a new point of insight, where the solutions of duty
are easy, and the otherwise perplexed questions
of casuistry are forever suspended; even as this
woman friend of Jesus saw more through her love,
and struck into a finer coincidence with his sublime
54   future, than all the male disciples around her had
been able to do by the computations of reflective
reason. Nay, if Judas who, according to John, was
the more forward critic, had been writing just then a
treatise on the economics of duty, her little treatise
of unction was better.

But we shall not understand either her, or the
subject we are proposing to illustrate, if we do not—
I. Bring into view the inherent difficulty that
besets all questions of casuistry that rise under the
laws, or precepts of natural morality. By casuistry
we mean, as the word is commonly used by ethical
writers, the settlement of *cases*, sometimes called
cases of conscience. The rules or precepts of morality
are easy for the most part, it is only their applications to particular cases that are difficult. And
they are often so difficult as to cause the greatest
perplexity in the most conscientious and thoroughly
Christian minds; as many of you will know perhaps
from the struggles of your own moral experience.
Ready to do any thing which duty requires, ready

to fulfill any precept, or law, which is obligatory, you have yet been tormented often with doubts, it may be, regarding what this or that rule of duty required of you, in the particular case which had then arrived. For the rules, or precepts of obligation, are all general or generic in their nature, while the cases are particular, and appear to even run into each other, by subtle gradations of color, so as to be separable by no distinct lines. Every case is peculiar, it is more, it is less, it is different—does the rule of duty apply?

55

Take for example, the statute "thou shalt not kill," either as a statute of the decalogue, or of natural morality. Under this, as an accepted law, there will come up, in the application, questions like these—Whether one can rightly be a soldier for the defense of his country? Whether he can rightly execute a criminal under the sentence of death? Whether it is murder to shoot a robber at one's bed-side in the night? Whether one can rightly defend a poor fugitive, hunted by his master, by assailing the master's life? Whether as a christian he may rightly pursue the murderer of his child, and bring him to trial, under a charge that subjects him to capital punishment? Whether he may order a surgical operation done upon a child, which there is much reason to fear will only shorten life? Whether he can run this or that considerable risk of his own life for purposes of gain, without incurring the guilt of suicide?

The same is true of any other main precept of

morality or statute of the decalogue. Accepting the law general, endless questions arise regarding its particular applications, which it seems impossible to solve.

Or we may take the great principle which requires doing good, the utmost good possible. And then the question will arise continually, in new forms endlessly varied; what is best to be done? And here we find ourselves thrown at every turn, upon a search that requires an immense fore-reaching, or impossible, knowledge of the future. What are God's plans in regard to tho future? shall we meet them and chime with them, by this course or by that? Or, if we only try to find what will be most useful, we can see but an inch for word, and how can we decide. Thus if the woman had been asking how she could use her box of ointment so as to do most good with it, she would either have fallen into utter doubt and perplexity, or else she would have taken up the same conclusion with Judas, and given it to the benefit of the poor. And so if you have on hand the question, whether, in the way of being useful in the highest possible degree, you will educate your son as a Christian minister? there come up immediately questions like these—Whether he will live to be of any service to the world? Whether he has talents to be useful? Whether he will maintain a character to be useful? Whether even God will make him eloquent, or keep him grounded thoroughly in the truth? A thousand unknown matters regarding his future, baffle you in coming to any intelligent solution of your duty. Any sort of business you propose to undertake as a way of usefulness, depends in the same way on a thousand unknown contingencies—the probable characters of partners and customers, the winds, wars, fires, seasons, markets of the years to come. In this manner you are brought up shortly, under the questions of duty, by the discovery that you can see hut a little way, whatever you propose, and that all your computations of usefulness or means of usefulness to be obtained, are too short in the run to allow the satisfactory settlement of any thing.

These difficulties, it is true may be exaggerated. Some men never have a trouble about duty in their lives, just because they have practically no conscience about it. Really conscientious persons, too, settle most of their questions as they rise, without debate. It is here exactly as it is in the law; for what is called the common law is a product of pure moral casuistry from beginning to end—ten thousand obligations are discharged without litigation to one that is settled by it, and yet the few to be thus settled are how many and troublesome. The reported volumes multiply till no one can read them, and yet the new cases come; the work is never done—never in fact to be done. Just so it is with our troubles of casuistry. The really conscientious man will be continually graveled by some question he can not solve by his reason, and one such question is enough to break his peace. However perfect and simple the code of preceptive duty, the

applications of it will often be difficult, and sometimes well nigh impossible, without some better
help than casuistry, which better help I now proceed,

II. To show is contributed by Christ and his
gospel. By him is added to the code of duty, what
could, by no possibility be located in it, a power
to settle right applications to all particular cases,
without casuistry, or any such debate of reasons as
allows even a chance of perplexity.

Thus, begetting in the soul a new personal love
to himself, practically supreme, Christ establishes in
it all law, and makes it gravitate, by its own sacred
motion, toward all that is right and good in all particular cases. This love will find all good by its own
58   pure affinity apart from any mere debate of reasons;
even as a magnet finds all specks of iron hidden in
the common dust. Thus if the race were standing fast
in love, perfect love, that love would be the fulfilling
of the law without the law, determining itself rightly
by its own blessed motions, without any statutory
control whatever. It is only under sin, where the
love is gone out as a principle, that we get up rules,
work out adjudications, creep along toilsomely into
moral customs and codes, contriving in that manner to fence about life and make society endurable.
These are laws that God enacts for the lawless and
disobedient; or which they, under God, elaborate for
their own protection. But who will go to love and
say, thou shalt not steal, or kill, or lie—does not love
know that beforehand? These decalogue statutes—

love wants none of them, she fulfills them before they are given. She can shape a life more beautifully by her own divine impulse, than it could be done by any and all ethical statutes, or refinements under them. And accordingly when Christ restores this love in a soul, it will be a new inspiration of duty, just according to its degree of power In so far as the love is weak, or incomplete, the fences of precept and rule will be wanted. But the now affinity it creates, ought to be so clear as to make all questions of duty more and more easy, till finally the sense of all such rules is nearly or quite gone by, leaving only the love to be its own interpreter and light of guidance.

Again it is a further consideration, drawing toward the same conclusion, that Christ incarnates a perfect and complete morality in his own person, so that when the soul in its new love embraces his person, it embraces, or takes into its own affinities, a complete morality. Consider who Christ is; the eternal Word of God for whom, and by whom, all the worlds were made; in whom as being in the form of God, all God's ends, creations, principles, counsels, providences, and future ongoings, are in a sense contained and totalized. Whoever loves him, therefore, loves in fact, all that he is in his perfection, and all that he means in the world, all that he is doing and going to do in it; and so loving him, all the currents of his soul run out with his, to meet as by a true inspiration, all his deepest purposes and most future and remotest appointments. He is in a state of mind that cleaves instinctively, and by hidden sympathies,

59

to all that is in the Lord's person. Where the reasons
of the understanding are short of reach, and ethical
solutions of all kinds doubtful, he is drawn by the
indivertible affinities of his heart, into easy coincidence with all that Christ means for him, and so into
a certain divine morality. He is not a philosopher, not
wise, as we commonly speak, and yet Christ, who
is being formed in him, is made unto him wisdom.
As the worlds are fashioned to serve His plans, and
work out, in the sublime progression of ages, all His
counsels of good, he falls into that same progression
to roll on with it, not knowing whither, and how,
and why, by any wisdom of the head, yet chiming
faithfully with all that Christ is doing, or wants to be
60   done.

   At the risk now of a little repetition, let us recur
a moment to the singularly beautiful example of the
woman, whose conduct gives us our subject, and
see how completely these suggestions are verified.
The wise male brethren who stood critics round her,
had all the casuistic, humanly assignable reasons
plainly enough with them. And yet the wisdom
is hers without any reasons. She reaches further,
touches the proprieties more fitly, chimes with
God's future more exactly, than they do, reasoning
the question as they best can. It is as if she were
somehow polarized in her love by a new divine
force, and she settles into coincidence with Christ
and his future, just as the needle settles to its point
without knowing why. She does not love him on
debate, or serve him by contrived reasons, but she

is so drunk up in his person, so totally captivated by the wondrous something felt in him, that she has and can have no thought other than to love him, and do every thing out of her love. To bathe his blessed head with what most precious ointment she can get, and bending low to put her fragrant homage on his feet, and wind them about in the honors of her hair, is all that she thinks of, and be it wise or unwise, it is done. Whereupon it turns out that she has met her Lord's future, as no other one of his disciples had been able; anointed his brow for the thorns, his feet for the nails, that both thorns and nails may draw blood in the perfume of at least one human creature's love. And this she has done, you perceive, because her life is wholly in Christ's element; tempered to him more fitly and totally than it could be by her understanding. By a certain delicate affinity of feeling that was equal to insight, and almost to prophecy, she touches exactly her Lord's strange, unknown future, and anoints him for the kingdom and the death she does not even think of, or know. Plainly enough no debate of consequences could ever have prepared her for these deep and beautifully wise proprieties.

Now in just this manner it is, that Christianity comes to our help, in all the most difficult, most insoluble questions of duty, those I mean which turn upon a computation of consequences. To compute such consequences, we need to know, in fact, a thousand things that belong to the future, and we know scarcely one of them—on what particular ends God

is moving, by what means he will reach them, what
effects will follow, or not follow, a supposed act of
usefulness, what trains of causes will be put agoing, what trains checked and baffled. Here it is that
our casuistry breaks down continually. At this point,
all merely preceptive codes are inherently weak and
well nigh impracticable. They command us to good,
or beneficence, and leave us to utter perplexity in all
computations of consequences that reach far enough
to settle the real import or effect of any thing. Nothing plainly but some inspiration, or some new im-
pulsion of love, such as puts the soul at one with
all God's character and future, as when it embraces
Christ and a completely incarnated morality in his
person can possibly settle our applications of duty
and give us confidence in them. Just what helped
the woman to come forehand in the anointing of the
Lord's body, is wanted by as all, at every turn of life.

And this I will now add, as a last consideration,
is what every Christian has found many times, if
not always, in his own experience. Thus, in some
trying condition, where he has not been able, by
the understanding, to settle any wise course of
proceeding, how very clear has everything been
made to him, step by step, by the simple and con-
sciously single-eyed impulse of love to his Master.
And when all is over, when his crisis is past, his
course fought out, his adversaries confounded, his
cause completely justified, his sacrifice crowned,
how plain is it to him that he has been guided by
a wisdom in his loving affinities, which he had not

in the reasons of his understanding; all in a way so easy as even to be an astonishment to himself. Not to say this, my brethren, out of my own experience would be to withhold a good confession that is due. And I can not persuade myself that any thoroughly Christian person is ignorant of the experience I describe. All our best determinations of duty are these which come upon us in the immediate light of our immediate union to Christ.

I ought, perhaps, to add that the doctrine I am wishing to unfold, does not exclude the use of the understanding. It is one thing to use the understanding *under* love, as being liquified and molded by it, and quite another to make it the oracle or sole arbiter of duty. Christ himself gives precepts to the understanding, just because we are not perfected in love, and require, meantime, to have the school-master's keeping, under a preceptive and statutory control. Nothing was further off from God's design than to add so many preceptive regulations by Christ and the apostles, to help out the natural code of morality, and be applied as that code is, and with it, by natural reason. He gives them only because we are not ripe enough in the good impulse of love to be kept right by that alone. We might take our passions for love, and become fanatics and fire-brands of duty. The false heats of our indignations against wrong, too little qualified by love, might fill us with personal animosities. Our lusts might steal the name of love and fool us by the counterfeit. Therefore he puts dry precepts in the understanding for a time, where, if they are legal and precisional in their way, the fogs of distemper and passion will be just as much less able to reach them.

Let me add now, a few distinct suggestions that crowd upon us naturally, in the closing of such a subject. And—

1. The great debate which has been going on for some time past, with our modern infidelity, is seen to be joined upon a superficial and false issue. The superior preceptive morality of the Gospel of Christ, which used to be conceded, is now denied, and the learned champions of denial undertake to refute our claim, by citing from the explored literature of the ancient Pagan writers, every particular maxim, or precept that we most value, or suppose to be most original, in the teachings of Christ. Which if they can do, as they certainly can not, their argument is only a very transparent sophistry. For, when they have hunted all treasures of learning through, picking up here one thing and here another, to match the teachings of Christ, and claim as the result, that they have matched every thing, their conclusions amounts to simply this, not that Christ is the equal of some man, but that he is just as competently wise as all men taken together. Besides they make him none the less original; for no one can pretend that Christ obtained, or raked together so many precepts, by any such hunt of learned exploration as is here resorted to; he mast have given them out of his own creative intelligence. And then again,

64

what signifies a great deal more, it is not here after all, that he made his grand contribution to the life of duty. The issue tried is wholly one side of his chief merit; viz., that he brings relief and clearness where all the natural codes of duty break down. These codes are grounded in natural reason, by that also to be applied. The chief maxims may be right, but the applications are still to be settled as no mortal man can settle them—by analogies, by subtle distinctions, drawn where there are no definite lines of distinction; by computations of usefulness depending on a knowledge of the future that is impossible. Every maxim wants a volume of casuistry to settle its application to this or that case in practice; and then new cases, equally difficult, will be rising still—even as they do at common law, which covers only a very small corner of the general field of duty. Baxter wrote an immense folio on cases of conscience, thinking, I suppose, that he had made, every thing clear to the end of the world; when in fact he had started more questions in doing it than twenty folios could settle. Handled in this way, the law of duty runs to endless refinements; and as men are corrupt, to endless sophistries and abortions; yielding codes in fact, that are codes of immorality, framing mischief by a law; codes of Jesuitry, codes of hideous and disgusting practice, such as heathen peoples propagate with endless perversity. How much then does it mean that Christ has a perfect morality incarnated in his person—all beauty, truth, mercy, greatness, wise counsel of life; so that when he is embraced, all casuistries are well nigh superseded, and the humblest, most unreasoning disciple, is able by a course of applications, wiser than he knows himself, to fill up a beautiful life, meet, with a glorious consent of practice, all the grandest meanings, and remotest future workings of God. The life of duty passes in a clear element, tossed by no perplexities, happy and sweet and strong, because the soul in Christ's love has a light of immediate guidance, In presence of this manifestly divine fact, how weak and sorry is the attempt to break down Christ's sublime superhuman evidences, by showing that his contributions to the mere preceptive code of duty, have been more or less nearly anticipated.

2. All conscientious Christian persons who get confused and fall into painful debates of duty in particular cases, may here discover the secret of their trouble and the way to have it relieved. Their difficulty is that they fall back on the modes of casuistry, and attempt to settle their question of duty, as Jesuits or heathens do, by computations of reason. Shall I do this? shall I do that? shall I give myself, or my son, or my husband to the army of my country? keeping one day in seven, how shall I keep it? training up my child for God, what indulgences shall I give, what pleasures shall I allow? having adversaries, shall I be silent? willing to make every thing a sacrifice for God, shall I give or not give all my time and talent to the immediate duties of religion?—ten thousand such questions are rising every hour, this with one

person, this with another. The debate is begun and
kept up day and night, till the soul is weary. The
darkness increases, the confusion grows painful, the
longer and more critical the debate is, till finally the
soul, thrown back upon itself, sinks into a kind of
nervous dread, close akin to horror. How many such
cases have I met, in past years, and they are among
the saddest to which I have been called to minister.
The question of duty was turned round and round,
till the multitude of reasons made distraction. It was
even as if duty were the only thing impossible to
be found. Have I any such afflicted soul before me
now? 0, my friend, that I could show you the root of
your difficulty. You carry your case to the wrong tri-
bunal, to the casuistries of ethics and not to Christ.
You get tangled in questions, when you should be
clear in love. Go where Mary went, or rather where
Mary's heart went. Cease from your refinements,   67
refuse to be caught any more in the mouse-trap questions and scruples of duty, and let it be enough to lay
your Soul on Christ's bosom. Resting quietly thus, in
the sacred bliss of love to Christ's person, wanting
nothing but to be with him and for him, your torment will soon be over. The question of duty will be
ended even beforehand, just because the soul of all
duty is in you. The current of your feeling will run
to it and settle it, even before you ask where it is.

3. It is no good sign for a Christian person, that
he is always trying to settle his duty by calculations,
and wise presagings of the future; and it is all the
worse, if he pleases himself in the confidence that he

succeeds. Doing nothing by faith, making no room for impulse or the inspiration of christian love, he takes the easy method of sagacity—easy to the fool as to the wise man—determining his questions of course mostly in the negative; for, if there is any doubt, it is always a brave thing, and always looks sagacious to say. No; and then, since he undertakes no duty which he can not see to the end of, even by his eyes, which is about the same as to undertake no duty at all, he conceives that he has a more solid way of judging than others. He will do nothing out of a great sentiment of course, he will break no box of ointment on the head of anybody; he will educate no son for the ministry, for example, lest possibly he should be only a martyr for the truth, and all that has been spent upon him, should only be anointing him for his burial. Meantime, what is the love of Christ doing in him? what great impulse of love does he trust enough to follow it? He makes a winter in the name of piety, and because nothing is melted in the heat of it, blesses himself in the solidity of his practice! Possibly there may be a little of the christian love in such a person, but the signs are bad. To be politic is no certain way of being good, and the man who tries it, perils every thing.

4. We have a striking, and at the same time, most inviting conception here given us, of the perfect state of society and character in the future life. Calculation, criticism, moral codes and precepts, none of these are wanted longer to regulate the conduct, all the legalities are gone by. There is no

debate of reasons, no casuistry. The reign of simple love has come. The impulse that moves has its law in itself, and every man does what is good, just because only good is in him. There is no scruple, no friction, no subtlety of evil to be restrained. The conduct of all is pure water flowing from a pure spring. And as springs are unconscious of their sweetness, thunders of their sublimity, flowers of their beauty, so the perfection of character and conduct is consummated in a spontaneous movement that excludes all self-regulation, and requires no dressing of the life by rules and statutes. All best and noblest things are done, as it were naturally; for Christ, who is formed within, must needs appear without in acts that represent himself. All acts of beauty and good are like that of the woman, coming to anoint her Lord—inspirations of the beauty she loved, wise without study or contrivance, unconscious, spontaneous, and free. This now is society, this is character; to this height of perfection, this blessedness in good, our God is raising all that love him.

69

After having sunned ourselves, my friends, in this bright picture above, some of you, it may be, will now return to the earth with a feeling more wearied and worn by duty than ever. This everlasting and compunctious study of duty, duty to children, husband or wife, duty to poor neighbors, and bad neighbors, and impenitent neighbors, duty to Sunday Schools, duty to home missions and missionaries, duty to heathens and savages, duty

to contrabands and wounded soldiers, and wooden
legs in the streets, and limping beggars at the door,
duty to every body, everywhere, every day; it keeps
you questioning all the while, rasping in a torment
of debates and compunctions, till you almost groan
aloud for weariness. It is as if your life itself were
slavery. And then you say, with a sigh, "O, if I had
nothing to do but just to be with Christ personally,
and have my duty solely as with him, how sweet
and blessed and secret and free would it be." Well,
you may have it so; exactly this you may do and
nothing more! Sad mistake that you should ever
have thought otherwise! what a loss of privilege
has it been! come back then to Christ, retire into the
secret place of his love, and have your whole duty
personally as with him. Only then you will make
this very welcome discovery, that as you are personally given up to Christ's person, you are going
where he goes, helping what he does, keeping ever
dear, bright company with him, in all his motions of
good and sympathy, refusing even to let him suffer
without suffering with him. And so you will do a
great many more duties than you even think of now;
only they will all be sweet and easy and free, even as
your love is. You will stoop low, and bear the load of
many, and be the servant of all, but it will be a secret
joy that you have with your Master personally. You
will not be digging out points of conscience, and
debating what your duty is to this or that, or him
or her, or here or yonder; indeed you will not think
that you are doing much for Christ any way—not

half enough—and yet he will be saying to you every hour in sweetest approbation—"Ye did it unto me."